JUN 09 1998

P9-CCS-831

Junebug

OTHER YEARLING BOOKS YOU WILL ENJOY:

YEARLING BOOKS are designed especially to entertain and enlighten young people. Patricia Reilly Giff, consultant to this series, received her bachelor's degree from Marymount College and a master's degree in history from St. John's University. She holds a Professional Diploma in Reading and a Doctorate of Humane Letters from Hofstra University. She was a teacher and reading consultant for many years, and is the author of numerous books for young readers.

For a complete listing of all Yearling titles, write to
Dell Readers Service,
P.O. Box 1045,
South Holland, IL 60473.

Junebug

ALICE MEAD

A YEARLING BOOK

Published by
Bantam Doubleday Dell Books for Young Readers
a division of
Bantam Doubleday Dell Publishing Group, Inc.
1540 Broadway
New York, New York 10036

If you purchased this book without a cover you should be aware that this book is stolen property. It was reported as "unsold and destroyed" to the publisher and neither the author nor the publisher has received any payment for this "stripped book."

Copyright © 1995 by Alice Mead

All rights reserved. No part of this book may be reproduced or transmitted in any form or by any means, electronic or mechanical, including photocopying, recording, or by any information storage and retrieval system, without the written permission of the Publisher, except where permitted by law. For information address Farrar, Straus, Giroux, 19 Union Square West, New York, New York 10003.

The trademarks Yearling® and Dell® are registered in the U.S. Patent and Trademark Office and in other countries.

ISBN: 0-440-41245-5

Reprinted by arrangement with Farrar, Straus, Giroux

Printed in the United States of America

February 1997

10 9 8 7 6 5 4 3 2 1

OPM

For Jeff and Mike, Larry and Luan

Junebug

One

I've got the sail hauled in tight. Lanyard's wrapped around my wrist. That sailboat leans over and just about flies out of the water, lifting high like a bird's wing. Foam and bubbles hiss past until there's a long, snaky trail behind us. I set sail for the West Indies, wherever they may be.

I don't really, though. Don't set sail for anywhere. Truth is, I'm just sitting in my seat, leaning my head against the wall of my fourth-grade class at the Auburn Street School, by the windows. That lanyard is the cord from the venetian blinds. It's Monday afternoon and I'm waiting for the three o'clock bell to ring so I can go get my little sister, Tasha, and head on home.

We're supposed to be finishing up a paragraph to hand in to Miss Jenkins, but I can't even get started. The only thing on my paper is my name and the title, "My Wish." Then nothing but thin blue lines.

I grab onto the cord one more time and look out the window. The wood along the classroom windowsills is old and yellow, and it has wavy black streaks underneath the shiny surface. I run my fingers along it. The windowsill's got lots of varnish on it, just the way sailboats have varnish on them, so the water won't rot the wood.

See? I know all about sailboats from those magazines Mrs. Swanson brings in to the project library. They come from a dentist's office. She's got so many she said I could keep some of them. Now they're under my bed in a big stack right next to my bottle collection.

Thinking about those bottles reminds me that I *do* have a wish. A birthday wish. And I'm going to put my wish on tiny pieces of paper, shove them into the bottles, and float them out to sea.

But my birthday wish is a secret. I'm hoping and hoping that it will come true. Until it does, I won't tell anyone about it. Especially Robert. He might make fun of me, so I'm not going to say one word.

I wrap the cord around my wrist. The wind's picking up. The seagulls are screaming overhead and the waves are going slap, slap, slap against the hull. Captain McClain yells to his crew. Shove over on the tiller and head into the wind! We're coming about!

The sails flap and crackle. I duck my head as the boom goes by.

"Junior!" says Miss Jenkins sharply.

4

"Huh?" I say.

Miss Jenkins's voice breaks through the sound of the gulls. She interrupts my journey. She's standing at the front of my row and it looks as if she just made some kind of announcement. Uh-oh. All the kids in my row are turning around, staring at me. But my buddy Robert, who sits in front of me, he's laughing, so I guess I'm not in real trouble.

"I said," repeats Miss Jenkins, "that anyone who didn't finish his paragraph should do it for homework."

"Oh. Okay."

I sure didn't finish mine, so I fold it up into a tight little square and shove it into my pocket. When the bell rings, everybody scrapes his chair back and heads on out, yelling goodbye to Miss Jenkins.

"Junebug," Robert says, out at the coathooks. "You gotta go get Tasha?"

Everybody except Mama and the teachers calls me Junebug, but my real name is Reeve McClain, Jr. Captain McClain to my crew, but they're invisible.

"Yeah, I guess."

"Oh, man." Robert shakes his head as if I just broke his heart. "Can't you leave her home?"

"Nope."

"Come on with me and Trevor downtown."

"Can't."

"Hey," Robert says. "Guess what I wrote about? I wrote about me being on the Knicks. Point guard.

I get down low. Dribble in under the basket when no one's looking. Sneak a shot. *Score!*"

"Oh, yeah?" I say back. "How come no one's looking? How come no one stuffed you?"

"Because I made it up just the way I wanted it."

I have to laugh.

"You make me mad, Junebug," Robert says. "How are you ever gonna get good at basketball if you don't practice with us down at the Boys' Club? How are you gonna impress the talent scouts when they start coming around?"

"I'm not. I'm not gonna play for no NBA. They can't afford me, anyhow."

Now Robert has to laugh. The crowd has thinned out. We get our jackets on and head down the stairs.

"Yeah? Well, you gotta be on the NBA if you want to be in a sneaker commercial," he says. "You know that one where King Kong walks through the city?"

He puts his arms out stiff and walks like King Kong down the stairs. I shake my head. He's one sorry case. Robert watches too much TV.

"Why can't your Aunt Jolita mind Tasha after school? I thought you told me that she'd babysit when she moved in with you all."

"I don't know," I say, shrugging as if I don't care. I don't want to talk about Aunt Jolita. "She's never around."

"Yeah? Well, you better quit hanging around five-year-olds. This is your last chance, Junebug," Robert calls out, running toward the front door to meet Trevor. "Are you coming or not?"

"Nah," I say. "See you."

Every day, Trevor comes over from the sixth-grade portable classrooms. He's waiting by the door for Robert. When he sees me, he shakes his head with disgust. I don't care. I don't like Trevor, anyway. Trevor's eleven, and he hangs out with some older guys at night. But I don't want to think about that.

I don't want to think about my birthday, either. It's coming in two weeks. May 18. And then I'll be ten. And that's when kids like Trevor start asking you if you want to go with them and maybe run some errands, earn some money. Somebody told me Trevor bought himself a gun. Maybe he did. Maybe he didn't. I don't know. Thinking about the gun, I feel sick to my stomach right there on the staircase to the kindergarten rooms.

"Don't think about it," I tell myself. "Don't." I shove the sick feeling away.

Some of the stuff that goes on in the Auburn Street projects, I'm never gonna do. These projects are like some kind of never-never land, like they never got put on a regular map. Nobody comes around here on purpose. It's as if we all got lost, right in the middle of the city.

The only person who comes to the projects by herself is that reading teacher, Miss Robinson. She comes after school to the room where Mrs. Swanson has a little library set up. That's where Tasha and I go after school sometimes.

I take a big breath. Then I run down the rest of the stairs.

All the kindergarten classes are down in the basement next to the rickety old bathrooms. Little kids have to go a lot, I guess, and the teachers don't want to have to be running all over the school looking for them.

There's Tasha, sitting in her cubby, waiting. I know she won't leave without me. She's got a round face just like mine; we're like two moons shining up in the sky. She sits there waiting, her lips pushed together and her brown eyes wide and still.

Some of the Puerto Rican families are still here. Sometimes a whole family comes to pick up one kid. Their mamas kneel down and shove those little kids' arms up their sleeves—poke, poke. Puerto Rican kids act all bendy and loose, like they're made out of Play-Doh instead of bones, getting all shoved and zipped, first one way and then the other. Their mamas kneel down and talk Spanish right up in their faces—fast, fast, fast. Spanish words come out like lightning. Makes me sound slow as a turtle. Then out they go. The mamas hold their hands, and the little kids kind of lean off to one side.

Tasha puts on her yellow windbreaker, slow and quiet. I reach up into her cubby and pull out her papers.

"These yours?" I ask.

She nods.

I glance down at them before I shove them into my pocket. No stickers today. Tasha doesn't usually get stickers, because she doesn't usually finish her work. I didn't finish my work today, either, but I have to as soon as I get home. Mama counts on me doing well in school, and I can't stand to disappoint her. How many times has my mama hugged me and Tasha and said to us, "You two are all I've got"?

"Come on, Tasha. Let's go."

She starts off up the stairs. She doesn't say a word. She can talk. She just doesn't.

TWO

Outside, I decide to check the alleyway behind the newspaper store. I'm looking for bottles to add to my collection, and I might find some back there under the dead leaves. I only collect glass bottles, not the flimsy, plastic kind.

But Tasha hates stopping for bottles. She breaks loose from my hand and runs and twirls in the wind. Her yellow jacket swirls out in a circle. Her barrettes are colorful as candy.

I run and catch up with her. She's usually such a slowpoke.

At the edge of the curb, where the weeds grow in summer, the gutter is full of shiny, shattered glass. Tasha squats down to touch it, and I slap her hand away before she gets cut. "That's sharp, Tasha. Leave it alone."

We have to cross two big streets, and then the big wide cement place in front of our building. A rusty, leaning-over sign says "Auburn Street Plaza," as if it were a fancy hotel or something. Believe me, it isn't!

Tasha hates that wide-open place. She looks down at her feet the whole time until I say, "Okay," right at the entrance. A rusty old fence runs around the sides of the building. There's supposed to be a playground out back, but there isn't.

I see my friend Darnell by the door. He's with some older guys, so I know I shouldn't bother him now. Darnell's the one who named me Junebug, way back when his mother used to babysit me and Tasha. He said I was just like a big old junebug, banging away at the window screens, pestering everybody with questions. Down in North Carolina, where Mama comes from, they have a ton of junebugs in the summertime, but around here they've just got me. Darnell likes to say that one of me is enough. He says I wear him out, but I know he doesn't mean it.

Darnell's fifteen. Mama says he's fifteen going on thirty.

"Hey, Darnell," I say.

He raises his chin at me to say hi as I go by. "Junebug, my man," he says and puts out his hand.

I slap him five, but I can tell he doesn't want me around right now.

Tasha and I go in through the lobby. It's a dark old cement-block place with nasty words spray-painted on the walls. We have to go upstairs to the ninth

11

floor. The stairs smell bad and sound all echoey and hollow. They vibrate, too. When someone's on the stairs behind you, you can feel them coming through your feet.

Tasha gets spooked in there, but Mama won't let us use the elevator. It's probably broken, anyhow. Usually is.

When we get to the ninth floor, I get out my key and unlock our apartment, 9-G. We go in and Tasha turns and slams the door. Then she bolts it. She almost takes my finger off, she shuts the door so fast.

"Nobody's gonna bother us, Tasha," I say. "You don't have to slam the door like that."

Wish I believed it.

We're standing in the living room. Couch, coffee table, TV, and us. Before Jolita came, Mama used to leave us a note every day on the coffee table. It always said that if we have a problem, we can call her friend, Harriet Ames, or Darnell's mother. Darnell's mother's home in the daytime because she works nights, and Harriet stays home to mind her grandson. But now, with Aunt Jolita supposed to be watching us, there aren't any more notes. No Aunt Jolita, either.

Tasha opens the refrigerator and looks for Kool-Aid. I come into the kitchen and watch her lift the plastic pitcher out.

"Anybody bother us, Tasha, and Darnell will take care of it. Don't you worry."

Tasha pours the Kool-Aid into two glasses. Lime-green. Then she puts the pitcher away and as she starts to sip looks at me as if she's wondering, Does that crazy Junebug know what he's saying, or is he just some big old dumb-dumb of a brother?

We lean against the table and drink the Kool-Aid. I don't know why school always makes me so thirsty, but it does. The Kool-Aid slides down quick. I put my glass in the sink the way Mama told me, and I go over to the living-room window. It faces due east, but that's nothing special around here. It looks right across the tar and fence out back. Across some nasty old train tracks that have no train on them.

You know the faraway place where the sky and the ground touch each other? It's not there. Instead, there's just a wall of old, smashed-up windows rising up to the sky. The embankment is piled high with dead leaves and trash stuck up against the fence. For a minute, I think I see a tall white bird crouched on thin legs in the leaves. But it turns out to be a plastic bag, empty except for windy air.

I asked Darnell about that building. He said it used to be the old Barrington gun factory. Shut down now, of course. Just like everything else around here, it used to be something, but now it isn't.

I go across the living room to my bedroom and put a few of my best bottles on my windowsill, including my old-fashioned green Coke bottle. Aunt Jolita said she'd bring me some more bottles. She said a friend of hers sells makeup and fancy soap, and her friend has all kinds of little bottles she can get me. She's told me that a couple of times, but I'm not holding my breath, waiting.

I get my head down low and look out across the city of New Haven, to where I *can* see the horizon. I look out through the ripply green glass of the bottles, and it's like looking through clear seawater. I think about sailing to a silky-smooth beach, pulling up my boat, flopping down on the warm sand.

I pull my homework paper out of my pocket and unfold it. I look at the title. "My Wish." I get a pencil, and I think about writing about being Captain McClain, sailing over the round blue curve of the earth. I think about writing about the silky-smooth beach, but I don't.

What good's a wish when you're turning ten and all around you is shattered glass? So I don't write anything. Not now. I toss the paper on my bed and head on out of the apartment.

Three

Most afternoons, we go down to the little library.
It used to be a storage closet full of buckets of cleaning supplies and brooms and stepladders. They took
that stuff out and put in some books and an old lady
from the Baptist church. She wears flowered dresses,
and she glares at us kids when we come in. She's Mrs.
Swanson, the one who brings boxes of old magazines
from a dentist's office. That dentist probably has a
sailboat.

"You treat the books nice in here," she says. "You
take care of them."

She thinks we have no manners because we live
here. Some older kids who come in here just look at
each other when she says that. She doesn't know our
mamas brought us up right.

That church lady, Mrs. Swanson, she's scared of all
the young men hanging out in the lobby with their
screechy girlfriends leaning on them. They play loud

15

music and they like to act rude when old people come by.

I go to the door of the library and look out. Jolita's out there with someone I don't know, but her friend's dressed to kill, with fancy orange fingernails and flared-out polka-dotted pants that swirl when she walks. Maybe that's Jolita's friend who sells the makeup.

"Hey, Jolita!" I call out.

She glances at me and narrows her eyes, wondering if I'm going to bother her or not. But I can see she's not in a bad mood. So I go ahead and ask, "Are you gonna bring me those bottles today?"

She lets out a big sigh of disgust and glances at her girlfriend.

"What's he want?" her friend asks.

"Some empty perfume bottles," Jolita tells her. "You think you deserve them?" she asks me.

"Definitely," I say. "Without a doubt."

"He's cute," her friend says.

"Not to live with he isn't," Jolita says. "All right. I'll bring them later."

Jolita and her friend head on out just as the reading teacher comes in. They don't say anything to Miss Robinson, and she keeps her eyes down, as if she doesn't want to hurt anybody's feelings. Then she sees me and Tasha, and she breaks into a big smile.

Tasha runs over to grab her hand, and the teacher calls out to me, "Hey, Junebug!"

Tasha leads Miss Robinson into the library. We sit at the little table. A couple of older girls, fifth- and sixth-graders, come here a lot, too, and use the crayons. They color real slow and careful, with dark outlines around everything. They always show their drawings to Miss Robinson when they get done. Some drawings she takes home. She says her refrigerator is covered with pictures.

Tasha brings a book and lays it on the teacher's lap.

"Now, what could this be?" the teacher asks Tasha, turning it over.

Tasha doesn't say a word, but that doesn't bother Miss Robinson one bit. "Hmmm. I wonder if it's the same book you brought me yesterday?"

Course it is. Tasha always brings her the same book.

"Why, look!" says Miss Robinson, acting surprised. "It's *The Tale of Peter Rabbit*."

Tasha smiles and leans against her leg. But it took her weeks to get there. Used to be that Tasha sat under the table while the teacher and I read books to her. Not anymore, though.

"After *Peter Rabbit*," says the teacher, "we're going to do something different."

That's good. I'm getting tired of that rabbit jumping into that watering can. He should have known better, if you ask me. I look inside the teacher's canvas bag. There's a lot of paper and markers in there.

Suddenly I hear loud yelling out in the hall, and swearing, too.

Mrs. Swanson gets up, all angry, and goes to the heavy metal door and shuts it. Then she goes back to her magazine. *Reader's Digest*. Sounds like something that happens to your stomach. I know she can't wait to leave.

But then I have to listen to the story. Peter Rabbit is running through McGregor's garden now. He's gonna get caught momentarily. Once old McGregor pops that basket over him, that's it. That rabbit ain't going nowhere. Then Peter gets sick and starts sneezing, and I ask, "Miss Robinson, are you a real teacher?"

Tasha glares at me. I know she's thinking, Here he goes with those pestery questions again.

"You work at the Auburn Street School, right?" I ask. I've seen her little red car there.

"I only work there one day a week."

"Is that all?" I ask. She's a good teacher. She ought to work more than that.

"I work at King School one day. That's it. Two days a week. I work at a grocery store at night."

"Where at?" I ask.

18

Tasha rolls her eyes. If she talked more, she'd tell me to shut up, but I'm not ready.

"Past the gun factory. Up Edwards Street," says Miss Robinson.

"You have to drive up there?" I ask.

Tasha puts her hand on her hip and smunches her eyebrows down. Mad.

"Yeah, it's a couple of miles away," the teacher says.

"You get paid to work here?"

"No, I don't."

Miss Robinson reaches down and starts pulling markers and paper out of her bag.

"Then what do you come here for?" I ask.

I can't help it, I want to know.

"Junebug, you hush up," Tasha says to me, all exasperated. I bet she's afraid the reading teacher will get sick of my questions and not come back, and then we won't have anywhere to visit after school.

But Miss Robinson smiles at me. "I know how to teach reading, and Mrs. Swanson's church put out an ad for a volunteer, so I came on over. And met you!"

"And Tasha," I add.

The teacher reaches into her bag and puts a brown spiky thing on the table. "I thought we'd make a book of poems," she says.

"Poems?" asks Tasha, her eyebrows arching up now.

"You know. Rhymes. Like in *Cat in the Hat*," I explain. "Hey, what is that thing?"

"It's a pinecone. From a pine tree."

"Must have been a big tree," I say. That pinecone is as tall as a coffee can.

But Tasha's looking confused. We saw some pine trees on a picnic up at the state park last summer. Mama and Harriet Ames love to go on picnics in the summertime. There was a bunch of pine trees in the grove by the picnic table. But maybe Tasha doesn't remember.

"Christmas trees have these," I tell her.

"That's a ornament?" she asks, even more confused.

"The seeds for a new pine tree are kept inside here," says Miss Robinson. "When the pinecone falls to the ground, the seeds fall out and a new tree can grow."

"Yeah," I say. "I knew that."

Miss Robinson folds a big wad of paper and creases it like a book. On the front she writes, "Poems are a magic carpet." Then she opens to a blank page.

"I brought something unusual on purpose. Stare into the pinecone as if it's a crystal ball. See what it tells you. What does it remind you of?"

Tasha reaches right out and takes it. She stares into the stiff little branches and turns it around.

"It looks like a brown-armed ballerina, twirling on

20

a stage." She whispers right near the teacher's ear so the big girls with the crayons can't hear.

Tasha says that because she wants to be a dancer. Miss Robinson writes it in big letters in the book. Then it's my turn.

I take the pinecone and stare at it. I feel loose, like when I'm looking out the window through the bottles, far away.

"It's a fountain of wooden water, spraying frozen time."

Miss Robinson looks astonished. Then she writes it down just the way I said it.

"I knew you two would be good at this," she says. "Anything else?"

Tasha thinks for a minute. Then she whispers, "I can fly."

Miss Robinson puts that in the book, too, while Tasha leans over her, watching. Then Tasha reaches out and points at the letters. Slowly she says, "I can fly."

Miss Robinson gives Tasha a big hug.

"Tasha," she says, "someday soon you're going to be reading *Peter Rabbit* to me."

Tasha doesn't say anything, but she's smiling a big old grin.

For some reason, I'm thinking about my homework. The empty page I left upstairs on my bed. I wonder if Miss Robinson could help me with that. It seems like I'm stuck. First I feel kind of hopeful, like maybe I could write a great paragraph. But right after that, I get angry. Seems that all teachers do, the nice ones anyway, is get your hopes up.

"Tasha's doing great, isn't she?" Miss Robinson asks me.

"Yeah," I say. "I guess."

I sit there staring at nothing, in a funny mood. Then I hear a voice. "Junebug!"

It's Jolita. She's at the door.

"Come here a second," she says. She glances at Mrs. Swanson, but doesn't come in.

Jolita's got her hands behind her back. This time she's with her usual pain-in-the-neck girlfriend, Georgina. Georgina's saying, "Come on. We don't have all day."

"All right. Hold on. Junebug, hurry it up," Jolita says.

She'll do just about anything Georgina tells her. I go on over to the door.

"Yeah? What?" I ask.

She brings her hands around front and opens them up.

"Ta-dah!" she says.

She's got four little perfume bottles, all different. I take them quick, before they disappear. One has little ridges cut in the glass, one is flared out at the bottom like a genie's bottle, one is round like a ball, and one is narrow and skinny.

22

I look up at Jolita. "Thanks!"

She starts to smile at me.

Georgina makes a disgusted noise and takes Jolita's arm. "Come on," she says. "We gotta go."

Four

Mama gets home after five o'clock. She works at a nursing home for the elderly and has to take the bus. Then she has to climb all the stairs, just like us. She says you never know who's going to get in the elevator with you. Same thing with the parking garages downtown. She won't go in those, either.

We get out the macaroni and cheese from yesterday, and hot dogs, too, while Mama changes out of her work clothes. She's not a nurse, but she's an assistant. She wears a badge that tells what she is, and she's got white sneakers that she cleans off every night.

Tasha and I help get the table set and pour drinks and everything. No matter how tired she feels, Mama makes us do it right. We can't even have the TV on while we eat. That's why Robert doesn't like to eat

24

over with us. He can hardly swallow unless the TV tells him how.

"Where's your Aunt Jolita?" Mama asks us finally.

We both shrug and sit down. Neither one of us wants to be the one to tell her Jolita wasn't here to babysit, as she's supposed to. And I don't want to mention that Jolita's been hanging around with Georgina. We watch Mama's face while she dishes out the macaroni and angrily slaps that spoon down on the plates.

Mama sits down to eat, but she kind of pokes at her food. Not too hungry, I guess. When Mama pushes her plate away and looks up, I say, "Guess what?"

Tasha runs to get a piece of paper and a pencil from next to the telephone.

"What?" asks Mama in a tired voice.

"You gotta guess," I say, bouncing on my feet.

She starts to smile. "We won TriState Megabucks?" she asks.

"Nope. Guess again!"

"Oh, Lord, I don't know."

"Tasha can read!" I yell out.

"Junior!" Mama says sharply. She doesn't want me making fun of Tasha, because the teachers told Mama that she learns slow.

"She can. Watch this," I say.

I write "I can fly" on the paper and pass it to Tasha.

"I can fly," she whispers.

Mama stares at her as if she doesn't believe it.

"Write something else," she says to me.

So I write "I can run" and Tasha reads that, too.

Then Mama gives Tasha a great big hug. She holds Tasha's round cheeks and rubs her forehead against hers. It looks like she might cry a little.

"Did she learn that in school?" Mama asks.

"Nope," I say. "That reading teacher who comes here in the little room downstairs. She taught her. Took awhile."

"You thank her for me," Mama says. "Be sure you thank her tomorrow."

I nod. "Okay." But I'm thinking, what would Trevor say if he knew I was hanging out, helping my little sister learn to read, instead of going out with the guys?

Mama starts clearing the dishes. I have to help scrape the plates into the trash. Tasha gets to go play.

"So, Junior, it's going to be your birthday in a couple of weeks."

"No way!" I say back.

"What are you talking about?" Mama looks at me. "You know it is. May 18. You'll be ten. What do you want for a present?"

"Corks," I say. "That's all I need. Corks."

"Young man," says Mama, "I do not understand you at all. That's what you want is corks?"

"Yep. They'll do the trick." I give her a big wide smile. Even Mama doesn't know my secret plan. Of course I need corks! How can you send a message in a bottle without a cork in the top?

Mama's standing at the sink now with her hands in the soapy water. She squeezes out a sponge and starts wiping the countertop real slow. I can tell she's thinking about something. She's had something on her mind since she asked us where Jolita was today. I'm getting a little nervous waiting for it to come out. Maybe I did something wrong. Seems like when you're a kid you're always doing something wrong. But I can't think what.

"My supervisor at work is going to be starting up a new program. Group apartments for the elderly, for the ones who aren't so sick. She asked me if I wanted to be a resident supervisor for a group."

"Where at?" I ask, frowning. What's going on here?

"Across town. You and Tasha would have to go to King Elementary."

Group apartments for elderly people? Now hold on.

"We'd be living with *old* people?" I ask, making a face.

27

"We'd have our own place. Smaller than this, though."

"Smaller?" I repeat with a squeak. Seems like I turned into an echo. How can any apartment be smaller unless it's a dollhouse and we're toys?

"Yes. Smaller," Mama says. "It would mean Jolita'd have to get her own apartment. We'd be on our own."

"Oh, man," I mumble.

I can't get all this straight. King Elementary is big. I've been there before. There's an indoor swimming pool over there, and the kids are a great big bunch of show-offs because they have the newest school in town. Besides, what about leaving my buddies here, like Robert and Darnell and Miss Robinson? I have to hang with my buddies. And what about Jolita? Where would she go? Are we just going to go off and leave her?

"Don't you want to move?" Mama asks.

"I don't know."

I never thought about it much. I never thought we could move. And didn't Mama say we'd be living with old people? I don't know about that. I really don't. Look at Mrs. Swanson. She's old. Old and mean! Imagine a whole apartment building full of Mrs. Swansons. What if we hated it there and wanted to come back? There's a two-year waiting list at the Housing Authority to get into Auburn Street Plaza. I'd be twelve years old by then.

"Aren't old people grouchy?" I ask.

Mama shrugs, wiping off the stove now.

"Some are. Some aren't. Just like everybody else."

She smiles at me. The counter can't get much cleaner. She's rubbing the holes right out of the sponge.

But now I'm thinking the other way. Maybe we should move. A swimming pool is almost like the ocean. A little square ocean smelling like chlorine. Maybe I could learn to be a good swimmer over at King. Maybe. And I could get away from Trevor and Georgina, and Trevor's gang.

But what about Jolita? She brought me bottles today. Maybe we could get to be friends.

"I don't know if I want the job. I've never been in charge of something like that. On my own. Managing elderly people is not always easy," she says. Then she sighs. "So I don't know. Something to think about, I guess."

After everything's cleaned up, I go over to the living-room window. There it is again. That ugly old gun factory. Rising up so high, it blocks the sky. I try to look way past it like I did with the pinecone, but words don't come. I see a big, dirty wall, shattered and busted up.

If we move, will it be someplace else just like this? Or will it be different?

Down on the tar, I see Darnell come out of the

back door of the building, walking slow. He kicks at a loose piece of tar, kicks it into the chain-link fence. Then he lays his head against that rusty wire and stands there. No older guys are with him now. Bet I can run down there real quick and see what he's up to.

"Mama," I holler, heading for my jacket.

"You don't have to yell," she says, coming out of the bathroom.

"Can I go outside and see Darnell?"

She frowns for a second because it's almost dark out.

"Yeah, I guess. But don't go wandering off."

"I won't," I call out, already out the door.

Darnell's mother used to be my babysitter, and Darnell likes to think he's my big brother, bossing me around, giving me his old toys, watching out for me. This past year, Darnell started growing like a weed. His sneakers are huge. Size 13. His hands are big, too. He's over six feet tall, bigger than his older brother, Gabe. Robert and I like to tell Darnell he's going to be NBA material, but Darnell says he's got other plans. I bang open the back door and run out to the playground.

"Darnell!" I yell. "What's up?"

"Nothin' much."

He glances at me and breaks off a hard little piece of smile. He tosses it at me like a coin. I gotta be quick and grab at it. He swats my head when I get closer, but I duck. He smiles again, a little longer this time.

"Your girlfriend break up with you?" I ask, wondering why he's sad.

He looks at me for a moment, as if maybe he's going to tell me something, and I hold my breath to see if he will. Then he just shakes his head.

"Nah," he says.

"Want me to go get Robert? We can play a little two-on-one. Robert's getting real good."

He laughs and shakes his head. Puts his face down close to mine. "No," he says. "Listen, Junebug, catch you later. I need to be alone for a while, okay?"

My face gets frowny. I bet I look like Tasha, but I can't help it. But I have to go. I respect Darnell, I always do what he says.

"Okay," I say.

I start to walk backward toward the door. He gives me one more little smile, then zips up his jacket and heads out front. I get the feeling the place he's going isn't much fun.

I go back upstairs to my bedroom. Tasha's playing doll babies on her bed. My side of the room is getting real crowded. My bottles are everywhere. I take the four new tiny ones into the bathroom and give them a good rinsing to try to get all that perfume smell out.

31

"Whew!" Mama calls from the living room. "What are you doing in there? Taking a bath in cologne?"

Those bottles sure do smell. I dry them off on the bath towel. Each one is cleaned and shined. No gooey labels stuck on them either. I set the new ones on my dresser and get to work on my notes. Nice, neat handwriting. I asked Miss Jenkins how you write to somebody you don't know. She said to put "To Whom It May Concern" at the top. So I already started putting that part on, even though it sounds terrible.

After I write a few notes, I line up my bottles from little to big. First the new tiny ones from Aunt Jolita. Then some hand-lotion bottles. Ketchup bottles. A.1. Sauce. A great big cider jug. All kinds of soda bottles.

I like looking at them. I can picture them in my mind, floating on top of the waves, each one carrying my secret wish to a far-off place. When I think about that and see it all happening, I don't feel so scared about turning ten.

These bottles are going to be my birthday flotilla. I'm just waiting on those corks.

Later I'm lying in bed, asleep. When I open my eyes, I realize I've been hearing Mama and Jolita's voices. Loud and angry. Mama's saying something about how Jolita never helps out, how she should help watch us kids if she's not going to get a job.

"You spoil those kids," Jolita shouts at Mama.

That makes me mad. She does not. I want to get out of bed and go protect my mama. Then, in the half-dark room, I see Tasha sit up and flip her covers back. I hear her sniffling. She slides across the floor in her bare feet, sucking on her two middle fingers and crying. I push back my covers and let her climb in.

She lies down and closes her eyes. I rub her back a little, the way I know Mama would if she didn't have to be up in the middle of the night, trying to set Jolita straight.

"You baby them! Junebug's almost ten years old, and what's he doing most of the time?" Jolita says, real loud. "Collecting bottles and hanging around his little sister, when he should be out with kids his own age."

"This discussion is not about my children," Mama says in a quiet voice. "It's about you helping out as part of this family."

I'm proud of my mama for saying that. Mama goes into her bedroom and shuts the door. Jolita goes into the bathroom, and I can hear the water running. A little later all the lights go out, but I lie awake a long time, worrying about everything in the world it seems, while Tasha lies next to me, sleeping through her dried-up tears.

And my last worry of all? I still didn't do my paragraph for homework. Guess I'll stay in from recess and get that done. First time I didn't do something I'm supposed to.

Five

Sure enough, at recess Tuesday morning, Miss Jenkins calls me over as the other kids run for their jackets.

"I know," I say before she gets a chance to speak. "My paragraph. I'll do it right now."

I grab a piece of paper and sit at a desk in the front row.

"Did you have a problem with the assignment?" she asks. "Do you need help with it?"

"No."

She picks up a stack of papers and her grade book. "Leave it on my desk when you're done." She's going down to the teachers' room. "Are you sure you're all set?"

"Yeah."

But that's not exactly true. What's the point of wishing for anything? Stuff that's never gonna hap-

35

pen. I guess I better write this fast and stop worrying about it. Here goes.

My Wish

I wish I had a sailboat that could fly me
over the water to a sandy soft beach where
X marks the spot. And when you dig down,
you find just what you wanted—diamonds
and treasure.

I leave it on her desk. I wrote it but I never once mentioned my birthday.

After school, everybody's hanging out around the outside of the apartment building. Tasha seems extra-nervous when we cross the open place. One time we heard gunshots there, that must be why. Some big fancy cars sit parked along Auburn Street. Everybody's playing loud music. I make Tasha hurry past.

"Don't you ever talk to people in those cars," I tell her. Since she doesn't talk much, it probably won't be a problem, but I have to tell her just in case.

The cars have tinted windows so you can't see in. A lot of bigger kids are hanging around them. I see Robert and Trevor over by the vacant lot, watching everybody. Then I see Darnell. He's walking toward a Mercedes. He's wearing a gold chain I've never seen before. The door of the Mercedes opens and a man in a dark suit gets out.

"Hey, Darnell," I call out, "what are you—" I want to ask him about that jewelry.

He glances at me and gives his head a tiny shake. I know he means for me to shut up. Darnell always told me, "If you're going to survive in the project, then you have to read people like a book." So I see his head shake and I shut up quick.

Stop asking questions, you old Junebug, I tell myself. Seems like I've been getting on Darnell's nerves lately. Tasha and I go on inside.

From the lobby, I can hear arguing out back on the tar. Loud voices. Girls yelling insults. Awful things. Inside the lobby, it's cool and tense, as if everybody hanging around is being extra-casual. As if they're all listening to the fight out back. I know I am. I don't recognize most of the voices, except for Georgina's.

We run up the stairs, and Tasha slams the door right behind us. Bang! This time, I don't tell her not to.

"Hey!" Aunt Jolita calls out, all sleepy, from the bedroom. She uses our bedroom during the daytime and the sofa at night. "What's all that noise?"

She sounds grouchy. Aunt Jolita and Mrs. Swanson ought to form a club. The Grouchy Club.

"You kids be quiet!" she calls out.

Tasha looks at me with a stubborn, sad look. It isn't fair for Aunt Jolita to yell at Tasha, because she hardly ever bothers anyone.

I go into the kitchen and pour the Kool-Aid, red

this time. Tasha sits in a chair to drink it. It's a long time until she can see the bottom of the glass, and I start thinking about last night, about Jolita telling my mother I have to grow up, when it's none of her business.

Then I think about Trevor and whether he has a gun. Robert says he got one to impress the older guys, to show everybody he's not scared. If they think he's brave, they'll take him into their gang. Because you can't make it on your own around here. You need protection from your friends. That's why you have to go with a gang.

I'm thinking about the names I see spray-painted on the walls. Death Posse. The Rex. Darnell told me to stay out of all that stuff. But just now, didn't I see him with that rich guy in the Mercedes?

"Come on, Junebug. Quit your staring," Tasha says, going over and tugging at the locks on the door.

I put my glass in the sink. She wants to go back downstairs to the library. I feel funny about going there today, though, with everyone yelling out back. Also because of what Jolita said last night, about me hanging around with a five-year-old. But I go on out the door, anyway. There isn't anything else to do.

I wonder if Miss Robinson will come today. Might be better if she didn't, with everybody keyed up in the warm spring air. I worry about her parking out front, then walking past all those teenagers pushing and shoving and bragging out at the curb. The only white person around.

When we get to the library, there she is, already at the table. Mrs. Swanson's there, and a couple of fifth-graders come in, too. Miss Robinson's brought a special reading book for Tasha and a game. Candy Land.

"Are you gonna play this, too?" I ask. I'm worrying about whether this is a baby game. I wish I'd never heard what Jolita said about me. Now it's as if I'm seeing myself from the outside, not the inside.

"Of course."

I nod and open up the game board. If the teacher's playing, I'm playing. The older girls come over. They want to play, too. They stack the cards up and we set up the plastic gingerbread men. Tasha sets hers on the lollipop forest instead of the starting place. Not a bad idea. I put my man on the ice-cream ocean.

Suddenly we hear terrible crying. A teenage girl named Evie rushes in, sobbing and grabbing her stomach.

"Hide me!" she cries. "Hide me!"

Mrs. Swanson jumps up, all angry. "You get out of here! Go upstairs right now and take your troubles with you."

"I can't. I can't," Evie says. She looks wildly around the room. There's no place to hide in here.

39

Evie runs to the door and slams it shut and locks it. "Don't tell anyone I'm here," she says. "You've got to help me."

She grabs the reading teacher around the neck, crying and holding on as if she's drowning. Miss Robinson holds her and rubs her back, trying to quiet her down and find out what happened. Already I hear angry voices outside. Evie hears them, too, and starts sobbing harder, all doubled up.

Miss Robinson takes her by the shoulders and looks in her face. "What happened? Can you tell me?"

Evie looks at me. "You know that friend of your aunt's? You know Georgina? We were downstairs earlier and Georgina said I called her a name. She said I made fun of her, but I didn't. She was yelling and yelling at me in front of my friends."

"Yeah," I say. That was the yelling I'd heard earlier.

"So later on me and my girlfriend, we knocked on Georgina's door. And when she answered it, we yelled out a name. Just fooling. And then we were going to run away. But Georgina pulled me inside. There were some other people in there, too. They were going to beat me up. They punched me."

Evie's crying again. "And Georgina, she bit me."

Miss Robinson opens the tear in Evie's blouse. There's a big bite place on her stomach. Miss Robinson takes a whole bunch of Kleenexes and puts it over the cut like a pad and presses on it, explaining to Evie that she has to hold it there.

Mrs. Swanson looks furious. She snatches up her purse. "I'm leaving," she says.

The kids all look at each other. She's gonna leave us in here alone? She heads over to the door. We can hear loud banging and yelling outside.

"Don't open the door," Evie begs. "They'll come in."

"Really, Mrs. Swanson. It's too dangerous right now," says Miss Robinson. "You've got to wait."

Mrs. Swanson sits on the edge of her chair and keeps her purse in her lap, as if she's waiting for a bus that's about to pull up.

All the time, the voices are getting louder. Shouting for Evie to come out and telling what they're going to do to her when she does. Tasha is crying. Miss Robinson is looking around the room, probably trying to think what to do.

"There's a phone in here," she says. "I'll call the police," she tells Tasha. "They'll come and help Evie."

I just look at her. It must be because she's white, she thinks the police are going to come. We've got two kinds of police—Housing Authority police and the regular kind. Neither one of them comes when we really need help.

Miss Robinson dials the emergency number.

41

"You've got to come," she's saying into the phone. "There are nearly a hundred people after this young girl. We're locked in a storage closet, five or six children and two adults."

She's begging and pleading with the police. Finally, she hangs up. Outside, men are pounding on the door, kicking it. All us kids stare at the door. Evie sits hunched over her hurt stomach, sobbing softly.

What if they break that door down? And what if they see a white person in here with us? They know Miss Robinson comes here all the time and plays with us. I feel bad doing it, but I move to a chair a little farther away from her, just in case.

It's been five minutes since she called, but it seems like a year. Miss Robinson picks up the phone to try the police again. I figure I have to tell her.

"They don't come by here much," I say. "Not when there's trouble like this."

She nods her head, understanding me. "But we have to call somebody. Who can help us? Everybody think."

Evie rocks in her chair, not saying a word. Then suddenly I remember that Aunt Jolita is upstairs in our apartment today, sleeping.

"I can call my aunt," I say to Miss Robinson.

Evie's head shoots up. "No!" she yells. "She's friends with Georgina. You know that."

I stand there, holding the phone. Maybe Evie's right. Maybe Jolita would help Georgina instead of me and Tasha. But then I remember the four little bottles she brought me, and I start to dial.

"Hello?" Jolita's voice still sounds sleepy.

I explain what's going on.

"What do you expect me to do?" she asks. "I can't stop an angry crowd like that."

"Just talk to Georgina. Get her to calm down."

"I can't do that," she says.

"Please!" I beg. "You've got to."

She doesn't say anything for a minute. Then she whispers, "Junebug, I can't."

"Then get Darnell for me. Get Darnell and his brother, Gabe."

"Yeah. Okay."

I hang up the phone, feeling as tired as if I just ran a mile.

"She's coming," I tell Miss Robinson, "with my friend Darnell."

Miss Robinson gives me a quick hug and a little smile.

I think of Jolita whispering on the phone as if she's scared. And she thinks we aren't?

People are shoving and arguing. I hear a body get slammed against the door. Then I hear a voice, loud but calm, asking questions. It's Darnell's voice, going on and on. And then the deeper voice of Gabe, talk-

43

ing, doing some agreeing. And then some laughing. Finally, I hear Jolita.

She knocks on the door.

"Junebug? Tasha? Excuse me? Are my niece and nephew locked in there, Georgina?"

I guess she isn't brave enough to tell Georgina that we called her on the phone. She's gonna pretend that she just now found out by accident.

I stand real still, thinking this. A hot, funny feeling runs through my arms and legs up into my face, and I realize I feel ashamed. For the first time, I feel ashamed of my own family.

I stand there frozen, but hot. I can't move. Until, finally, I kick that Candy Land boxtop across the room for no good reason except that it got in my way.

Outside, it's getting quiet, and when we finally open the door and peek into the lobby, there's nobody there. Not a soul. The way after a storm the clouds blow away real quick. It's hard to remember it happened at all.

Mrs. Swanson pushes past me. Evie runs upstairs to call her mother.

"That's it," Mrs. Swanson says to Miss Robinson. "As of today, the library is closed. I refuse to stay here anymore. I'll tell the church. The reading program is over."

And out she goes. Doesn't say goodbye to us or anything. As if it were our fault. And we never once were rude to her.

"Well," says Miss Robinson, looking around with her arms at her sides. Her arms probably got tired from holding Evie all that time. "Well, I guess I'd better leave, too."

The lobby is quiet as a graveyard. I'm thinking about how we don't have a library anymore.

"Lucky Tasha can read already," I say. "She learned just in time."

Miss Robinson bursts out laughing and bends down to look at me. "I'll miss you, Junebug," she says.

"What day are you at the school?"

"Thursdays," she says.

She's putting Candy Land back in the box. So much for the gingerbread men and the ice-cream floats. I don't help her because that way it takes her longer. Tasha and the other kids don't help, either.

She picks up her canvas bag, but her face is nervous now. She looks quickly out the door. I bet she's afraid of being a white person walking through that lobby today. But she goes to the door and smiles at us, anyway.

I jerk my head away to hide my sudden tears. Every time, it seems, every single time you think you've got something going for yourself around here, it slips away from you fast. That's what this project does. All at once, for no reason, things change. You can't count on anything. Nothing stays.

She hugs both of us goodbye and walks out to her car. She can drive away, but we have to linger behind.

Six

Next afternoon, we're drinking Kool-Aid, red again, and Aunt Jolita's sitting on the sofa, watching soap operas on TV. She told Mama she'd watch us.

"Why don't you two go on outside?" she says.

I guess she watched us already. An ad comes on. Aunt Jolita grabs the remote and flicks to another channel.

"Go on, I said. Out."

She never even looked at us. Isn't this our apartment? Mine and Tasha's? It sure ain't hers. She doesn't even help out with the rent.

Slowly we go down the stairs and out in front of the building. The sun is bright and warm again. Summer's coming for sure. And that means my birthday's coming soon, too. Maybe I could drink some shrinking potion, but who has some?

I see Darnell out front. He looks around, then wanders over to us.

"Junebug," he says.

"Darnell," I say back.

"Your Aunt Jolita home for once?"

"Yeah," I say.

"Send Tasha on up. You have to come with me."

"Where at?"

"Never mind that. Tasha, you go on upstairs. Go on."

Seems like nobody wants her around today. She looks at me for help, but it seems like I have to go with Darnell.

Tasha drags herself back toward the doors, looking pitiful. She's good at it, too. I almost go after her.

"Come on," says Darnell. "She'll be fine. Nobody's going to mess with Tasha. You can't watch her every minute, anyway."

He starts walking toward the empty lot next to our building. Burned-out cars sit in the lot, with no tires on them. Riding on rims. Weeds poke up all over the place. There's a shopping cart somebody pushed all the way from downtown. No grocery stores near here, that's for sure.

"Junebug!" someone yells.

I turn around and see Robert waving at me from the sidewalk. He's holding up a basketball and pointing at it. That kid's got one thing on the brain.

"Come on!" he yells. "Get over here!"

"I can't!" I yell back. "I gotta go."

I turn around and chase after Darnell. "Where are we going?" I ask, running to keep up.

We climb through a hole in the rusty wire fence. We're standing on the old railroad tracks. The empty gun factory is rising up on one side of us. The project's rising up on the other.

"Junebug," Darnell says, "you ask too many questions."

He walks on the big railroad ties lying crosswise. He steps over the stones in between.

"I know," I say. "That's just my nature."

Darnell gives a laugh and keeps on walking. "How old are you?" he asks.

"Nine."

"Yeah. That's what I thought. Today, you're getting an early birthday present."

"That's okay, Darnell. I don't need any present. Don't need a birthday, either."

"What are you talking about?"

"I ain't turning ten."

"Oh yes, you are."

"Uh-uh. You got it wrong. Just pass me the shrinking medicine."

"Junebug, you are one crazy kid."

We walk on down the tracks. On and on. Old beat-up factories on both sides. A nasty stray cat stares at us, then ducks down in the weeds. I've never been this far before.

"Darnell." I stop walking. "Where are we going?"

"Not too much farther. I got something to show you."

"Yeah? Well, you can show me right here."

"No I can't. It ain't in my pocket."

He's walking faster now and I have to run to keep up. Darnell's got long legs. I guess they go with his big feet.

Pretty soon, we come to a bridge where a road crosses over the tracks. Darnell climbs up the bank. "Come on," he says.

I follow up. The loose dirt crumbles and rattles downhill under my sneaker treads as I scramble up beside him. We sit all huddled up, under the bridge. Nobody can see us.

"So?" I ask. I don't get it.

"Look at this," says Darnell.

He lies down flat and wriggles his shoulders and his butt sideways through a narrow hole, like a letter going through a slot. He disappears under there.

"Come on," he calls out to me.

Here goes nothing, I think, as I wriggle and squirm in, too. Darnell's got a flashlight on, so I can see, or I would have been some scared. It looks like a cave carved out of dirt. A hideout. But you can't sit up. The roof's not high enough. I hope there aren't rats. I do not like meeting rats.

"Are we under the road?" I ask.

"Yeah."

"Did you make this?"

"Nope. Somebody showed it to me once, like I'm showing you. This is a secret, Junebug. You can't tell anybody. Not the reading teacher. Not Tasha. Nobody."

"Yeah, okay."

I nod my head, but I have a sick feeling in my stomach, the one I get when I think about Trevor and his gun. And I feel some big questions coming on. Why was Darnell standing by the fence yesterday, looking sad? And why does a fine boy like Darnell have to be lying in the dirt in the first place?

"Darnell, why are you showing me this?" My voice is shaking a little.

I think I already know the answer, but I just want to make sure.

"Because I'm going away, that's why. You're gonna have to get someone else to help you out when you get trapped in the library."

He smiles at me. But I can't smile back. Darnell, going away? I have tears in my throat. Tears everywhere.

"Why are you going?" I ask, my voice sounding croaky.

"I gotta go. You know that. What am I going to do? Stay here?"

Darnell slides his hand into his pocket and pulls

51

out a big bunch of money. I've never seen so much money. Looks as if Darnell turned himself into a bank.

"I ain't coming back, Junebug."

"Where'd you get that money from, Darnell?"

"Never mind."

"From a store?" I ask. I don't want Darnell to be a robber.

He laughs a little. "It's not from a store."

"Okay." I believe him. "But from where, then?" I have to find out.

"I've been saving it up. Plus I ran some errands for somebody."

"What happened to that gold chain you had?"

"I sold it."

I'm thinking now—about the gold chain Darnell had, about the man in the Mercedes.

"Who'd you do errands for? That man from yesterday?" I ask.

He puts the money back in his pocket. "You gotta know everything, don't you? Yeah, him," he says.

Then he pulls out a card. It says State of Connecticut driver's license across the top. Picture of Darnell on it, too. But not his name.

"This is so I can get a decent job. It says I'm eighteen."

"But you're only fifteen!"

"I know, but you have to be eighteen for the good jobs."

"You mean you're not going to school anymore?"

"I can't, Junebug. Not right now. This is like a war, living here. Pretty soon, they're gonna come after you. And then you have to take sides, for your own protection. Once you sign on, you're in the war."

"No way. I'm not going to."

"Yes, you will. What choice do you have? This is a real live war, but it ain't on TV. Nobody's winning it, either. We're just fighting ourselves."

I think about this for a minute. "Does Trevor have a gun?" I ask.

"Trevor?" Darnell gives a short laugh. "Yeah."

I lay my head down on the dirt. It's cool and grainy on my cheek. Doesn't feel so bad, after all.

"That money's my ticket to freedom, Junebug. You have to buy your way out of here. No Harriet Tubman's gonna come down and lead you by the hand."

I close my eyes. I see a map. But the map's all blank. No directions. Nowhere to go. I open my eyes and draw a big X in the dirt.

"Know what I call the project?" I ask.

"What?"

"Never-never land."

Darnell laughs. Then he says, "You ever get in trouble or someone's looking for you, you can hide here. Nobody can find this place."

He shines the flashlight around inside. He's got a pile of comic books and some cans and a couple of

53

plastic bags to lie on. All of a sudden, I can feel Darnell leaving me. I close my eyes again, all dizzy, it hurts so bad. Darnell's the closest I've got to a father.

"Junebug?" he says.

"Yeah?"

"Don't tell anybody you saw me today."

"I won't."

Course I won't. What does he think I am? I frown at him.

"Is this my present?" I ask.

"Yeah."

"Thanks."

"Now you get out of here," he says. "You get on back to your babysitting job."

I start to squirm sideways out of the hole.

"And, Junebug?"

"Yeah?" I stop and look back at him.

"Your Aunt Jolita, she's hanging out with a bad crowd. Her friends are into all kinds of stuff. Stealing and drugs. So you be careful."

"Yeah, okay. Bye, Darnell," I say in a sad, small voice.

I climb out of the hole and slide down the embankment. I start back along the tracks by myself. Without Darnell around, I feel as if I've lost my way already. I knew, before, he was always there to keep me safe. Not anymore. Now I have to keep myself safe.

Tears are sliding all over my face. I think about

Trevor and his gun and Jolita's nasty friends. It's too much. My nose is running and I wipe it with the back of my hand. I just walk on, my feet leading the way, leading back to Auburn Street, where I don't want to go.

Maybe Mama should take that job with the old people and we should leave, too. Maybe. And go to a school where I don't know anybody and Tasha doesn't either. And what if the job doesn't work out? Then maybe we'll be homeless. I know kids who are homeless, living out of cars and motels and stuff.

I stumble on. I'm not looking at the tracks, not seeing anything around me. Instead, I hear the seagulls hollering overhead and the sail snapping in the breeze. My boat rocks up over the waves like a freed horse galloping. The cool salt spray settles on my arms and face. I readjust my hat with the gold braid. Captain McClain is holding that sail tight, riding the waves, heading for the West Indies, wherever they may be.

That night, somebody knocks on the door real loud, about nine o'clock. I've just gotten into bed when I hear it.

Aunt Jolita is all dolled up, ready to go out. She opens the door. I peek out of my bedroom.

A man is standing there in a fancy suit, felt hat, holding leather gloves, looking like Eddie Murphy when he wears a tuxedo. The man steps inside without being asked. Two men wait behind him in the doorway.

"Hello," the man says to Jolita.

Mama rushes out of her bedroom. "Who said you could come in?" she asks.

"Is Junebug here?" the man asks, turning his dark glasses one way, then the other, like he's radar, scanning for me.

I don't want Mama to have to lie about me, so I come right on out of my room.

The man sees me. "You know Darnell?" he asks.

"Yeah," I say in a babyish voice.

"You see Darnell today?"

"Nope." I shake my head.

"Listen, if you see him, I want you to come tell me right away. I've got some money for you. He's got something of mine and I need it back. You understand?" He lifts up his dark glasses and stares right at me.

"Yeah," I say. "Okay."

My heart starts beating faster. Darnell took some of that big pile of money from this guy. But the guy must have owed it to him. Darnell would never take something he shouldn't.

"You friends with Trevor?" the man asks suddenly.

"Trevor?" I ask, trying to act confused. "Yeah, a little."

I feel like he's taking an X-ray of me, of my insides. And he's gonna take that little X-ray with him to use later on. I hope he doesn't see my heart beating like a crazy drum inside me.

Then he puts on his dark glasses and flaps his gloves at the other two men, and they all leave.

"You're not going out with him, are you?" Mama asks Jolita.

"Why don't you stay out of my business? You're already running my life for me enough as it is," Jolita says.

About a minute later, Jolita leaves, too, closing the door hard behind her. Not slamming it, but almost. Mama and I sit on the sofa.

Mama looks real tired. "Why are they looking for Darnell?" she asks.

"I don't know."

"Yes, you do," she says. "Don't lie to me, Junior."

"Darnell's leaving. He's not coming back."

"Does his mother know?"

I shrug, holding out my open hands.

Mama nods and then lays her head back against the couch, as if it got too heavy to hold up.

"Don't you ever take money from that man. You hear me?"

"I won't."

She's told me this a hundred times already. But isn't money the ticket to freedom? Isn't that how you book a flight out of never-never land?

"Mama?"

"What?" She rolls her head sideways to see me.

"Are we gonna be moving?"

"You mean, am I going to take that new job?"

"Yeah."

"I don't know. Seems like I'm barely managing the job I've got," Mama says, her hands lying limp in her lap.

I get shivery and scared, sitting there, looking at her floppy hands. Hands aren't supposed to look like that. They look a lot better when they're busy doing things, instead of lying around like caught fish.

"How come Jolita doesn't help out more?" I ask.

Mama sighs and gives a tiny shrug, I guess too tired to lift her shoulders up high.

"I guess she doesn't know how."

That isn't much of an answer, but I don't dare ask again. I hurry back to bed and climb under the covers.

I can't stop thinking. I hope Mama isn't giving up. She can't, or else what's going to happen to me and Tasha?

I lie there, staring at the dark ceiling. I hear Mama moving around, slowly putting stuff away, straightening up before she goes to bed.

Seven

Next day, we're out on the playground during recess when I see the reading teacher pull up in her red car and get out with her big canvas bag.

I go running over to the fence. "Hey, Miss Robinson," I yell.

She gives me a big smile. "How are you?" she asks.

"I'm all right."

I start to turn around.

"Wait a second," she says. "I have something I want to give you."

"For my birthday?"

"When's your birthday?"

"Next week."

She reaches into her bag and pulls out the poetry book that we started. She hands it to me. "I know we didn't get very far, but maybe you can finish it on your own. And you can remember the fun we had."

She comes through the opening in the fence and starts to walk with me toward the school. The end-of-recess bell rings. I bet I'm gonna be late.

"You like writing poems?" I ask.

"Yes. I like thinking about things and writing down what I think. It makes me feel free. Like when we wrote about the pinecone."

"Is that what you do all the time, write poems?"

She laughs. "That would be nice."

"I better hurry up," I say.

"Me, too," she says. "Bye, Junebug."

She runs up the front steps with her canvas bag. The heavy school door closes behind her as she disappears. I sink down on the steps, about to cry. Instead of going back to my classroom, I turn around and walk home. Tears in my eyes make the glass in the gutter sparkle like diamonds.

I wander slowly all the way home, kicking stray pebbles. My stomach is knotted up inside. There's too much going on. Darnell leaving and Jolita and Mama having an argument and the library closing. And I hate all of it.

It's the middle of the morning. The project's quiet this time of day. The kids are at school. Other people are at work. And the party crowd is still sleeping. I wonder if Aunt Jolita is asleep. Probably. I go around back and sit up against the wall, where it's sunny. I lay the poetry book down on my lap and stretch my legs out.

Why do people keep on giving me empty stuff? Empty hole, empty book. Upstairs I have a pile of empty bottles, each one waiting for a slip of paper and my birthday wish.

I have another wish, too. I wish I had a magic carpet. I'd fly right up and over that wrecked gun factory. Past the broken windows, over the ugly roof. On the other side, I bet there's . . . I don't know.

What did that teacher say? Let your mind go free? Sounds like a song on an album Mama has. Aretha Franklin. She has a voice that goes free, soaring up high like a kite, like the top of a roller-coaster ride.

If I let my thoughts go free, they're gonna run smack into that ugly wall of the gun factory. Or smack into Aunt Jolita. Or into that metal door where the library used to be. Locked up. That's what I am. Locked up in never-never land.

And who's got the key?

I don't know. So why don't I make a third wish? Why not? It's not gonna cost me anything. I open the little poem book and write, "I wish I wasn't locked up."

I remember that the worst thing of all yesterday was looking at my mama and thinking maybe she was going to give up.

Giving up is the worst. That's why Trevor got himself a gun, because he already gave up trying to be himself. All he can do is go with a gang. Going with a gang is giving up. I swear I won't ever do it. I swear.

I get to my feet.

But what am I going to do instead? I look at my scraggly little writing in the poetry book. I wish I could have shown my bottles to the reading teacher. I was thinking maybe she and Darnell could have come to my party. But I guess now, for sure, I won't have one.

I unlock the door to the apartment, and there she is! Well, what did I expect? It's big old nasty Aunt Jolita, as usual. Her hair in rollers. Big slippers on her feet. Smelly old coffee cup, all stained, in her hand.

But instead of using her grouchy voice she says kind of soft, "What's up, Junebug? What are you doing home this early?"

"Nothing. Got a stomachache." I drop the poetry book on the floor.

"You sick?" Jolita asks.

I'm not really sick, but I'm not my usual Junebug self, not by a long shot. "Nah. Maybe."

I flop down sideways on the sofa, my stomach hanging over the armrest, head on the cushions, feet on the floor. Jolita goes off to call the school and tell them I don't feel well. Then she comes over to the sofa.

"Come on. Sit by me." She pats the sofa next to herself.

I don't want to sit by her. But I pull myself up, all reluctant, and drop down in the seat next to her anyway.

"What's this?" She picks up my book and flips through it.

"Supposed to be poems and wishes, but it ain't."

She reads the first page. She reads how Tasha wants to be a ballerina, twirling on the stage.

"Tasha wants to be a dancer?" she asks, surprised.

"Yeah."

"Why didn't she tell me that?"

I shrug. "How come you never asked her?"

"You know what, Junebug?" Aunt Jolita sits forward, bright-eyed, and looks at me. "I used to want to be a dancer, too, when I was little."

"Yeah? Maybe that's how come you go to parties all the time."

"Maybe," she says. "I never thought of that. You know, you're a smart boy."

"Can't get smart with the library all locked up," I say, looking right at her.

She doesn't answer.

"How come you're friends with that dumb Georgina, anyway? If she hadn't started that fight with Evie, they might not have closed the library."

"Oh, Junebug. Seems like fights around here just happen every so often. It doesn't much matter who starts them. People just get mad. They've had enough of this place. You know that feeling."

"Yeah, I do," I say. "But I don't bite anybody."

I wonder how come Jolita and I are talking like

this. It must be because of the wishes. Maybe they make people brave.

"What else did you wish for?" I ask, feeling more like a junebug again.

"I wanted to be a movie star."

She drinks some coffee and looks at me over the top of the cup to see if I'm laughing at her.

"Then how come you aren't one?" I ask.

She shrugs and puts the cup down. "Didn't know how, I guess."

Then she stands up. "I have to get dressed now." She takes her things into the bathroom.

I don't get it. Doesn't she care anymore? Doesn't she care that she's not a movie star? I go into my bedroom and stand there a minute. My bottles are lined up in a long, winding line like a glass snake. Time for me to write some notes. It's not much longer before the launching.

I sit down and start to write: "To Whom It May Concern. My name is Reeve McClain, Junior, and for my birthday wish I would like to sail a boat. You can find me at 686 Auburn Terrace, New Haven, Connecticut, U.S.A." I have to write that fifty times because I'm going to launch fifty bottles. And, sure as heck, somebody has to find one of them.

That night, at supper, Aunt Jolita is acting bossy and superior, the way she usually does. I'm sitting on the sofa with my magazines, watching her rush around. She tries on one set of earrings after another. She puts on some big round plastic white ones.

They look fine. She looks in the bathroom mirror, then yanks them off and storms over to her jewelry box on Mama's dresser. She grabs some gold hoops and puts those on. They look fine, too. What's the big deal? Then I start thinking, she sure has a lot of earrings, considering she has no job or anything.

"Tasha, would you mind?" she says. "Why do you have to have your dolls under here?"

Tasha's got a bunch of her stuffed toys under the dresser, camping out or on a field trip or something. Jolita bends over and takes her shoe and sweeps them all out of there. Tasha doesn't pick them up. She leaves them in a pile in the middle of the floor and goes to sit in the rocking chair.

Mama got home late and is too tired to make anything special for dinner, so she's opening a can of baked beans. That's okay with me. I like baked beans. I put a ton of ketchup on them.

Now Jolita's fussing with her hair. Her hair's fine; it's herself that isn't. She's in my bedroom, using the hair dryer, when she yells at me. "Junebug! These bottles are driving me nuts. Get them out of here."

I hear her kick a couple. They clank when they fall down and knock together. She'd better not break any, that's for sure, or I'll get Darnell to— No, I won't either. I forgot.

"Who are you going out with?" Mama calls out from the kitchen.

"Excuse me?" Jolita comes out of my bedroom, holding the hair dryer, the plug dangling. She gives Mama a look that says no way is she going to answer that.

"Come on," mutters Mama to us, ignoring Jolita. "Time to eat."

She slaps those plates down in front of us. Baked beans and another hot dog. Carrot sticks. She moves into the kitchen, her back stiff. I can tell she's angry. Tasha and I keep our heads down low to eat, staying out of trouble.

We finish fast and start scraping those plates. After I help with the dishes, I lie on the sofa with my sailing magazines, looking at them. The water's so blue in the ads you can hardly believe it. Foam curves back from the bows, crisp and aqua. My favorite is a picture of boats with big colorful balloony sails out front. Spinnakers. They look like clouds of rainbows puffed out.

On the back pages are ads for catalogues that sell boat-building plans. Someday I might send away for some plans. But it costs three dollars just for the catalogue, so I haven't decided yet.

There's someone banging on the door. Aunt Jolita unbolts all the locks and yanks it open. There's that same man, the guy with the Mercedes and radar vision, with his gloves, hat, and big dark glasses. His teeth gleam at Jolita. He's sleek as a wild animal.

"You ready?" he asks, smooth-voiced.

Mama rushes over to Jolita. "Just where do you think you're going?" she asks loudly.

"None of your business, girl," says Aunt Jolita.

No one calls Mama "girl" like that and gets away with it. Aunt Jolita brushes by Mama, wearing her red sequined top, tight black pants, gold hoops. High heels clicking.

"Excuse us for a minute," Mama says to the man. "We need to talk."

She takes Jolita's arm, but Jolita yanks her arm away. All her bracelets jangle.

The radar man isn't smiling now. Looks like he's going to give Mama about ten seconds and that's all. Mama starts to say something, but Jolita pushes past her and rushes out the door to the landing. She hurries down the stairs. The man takes Mama's arm and starts to shove her back into the living room.

"Jolita!" Mama calls out, twisting away, free of his grasp. She runs out to the landing.

But the man grabs her again. He won't let go this time. Mama twists her arm hard and pulls free with a jerk. Then she gives a little cry, and she trips and tumbles backward down the stairs. I can't see her anymore. The man leaves, his shiny black shoes tapping down the cement stairs real fast. I hear a door close. Jolita and the man are gone.

"Mama!" I yell out.

She's lying in a heap at the bottom of the next

landing. She doesn't answer at all. I fly down the steps, my knees shaking. I'm crying a little high-pitched whimper.

I touch her. She's warm and soft, same as always. But she's too soft. Her arm lies there limp.

"Mama?"

Tasha is crouching behind me, grabbing hold of my T-shirt. Mama's just lying there as if she's had enough. She can't be bothered to try anymore. She gave up and went away someplace and left us behind, alone.

But she can't give up! I won't let her. I run upstairs to the phone to call the ambulance. Tasha stays on the landing by Mama, her eyes round and her mouth tiny.

I call the ambulance and the police, too. But they say they have a busy night and it's going to be awhile. Then I have to tell Tasha to go get Harriet Ames, Mama's friend, by herself, because I have to run out in front of the building to show the ambulance where to go.

I'm shivering with cold out there in the dark, with just my T-shirt on and no jacket. The wind's blowing right in under my shirt. I'm shivering so bad that my teeth are chattering and my body's jerking from side to side, and it's May. Not really that cold. But I am. I'm freezing and it seems that the ambulance won't ever come. I hate to leave Mama up there on the floor like that. I hope she won't wake up and find nobody there to help.

They gotta hurry. Those rescue people have to get here soon.

It seems like forever, but finally they come and lay Mama flat on the stretcher. Her eyes flicker open a little bit, but she doesn't say anything, and she has to go in the ambulance all alone. She's pushed in on the stretcher and then the two big doors are shut tight. I hope they're shut tight. I hope she can't roll out the back. Then she'd be lost forever. I forget what hospital they say she'll be at. I keep nodding and crying, and the rescue people think I understand, but I don't

I stand out on the wide cement place and watch the red flashing lights of the ambulance pull away in the dark with my mama. I never before felt such a big hole inside. Never.

Eight

Upstairs, Tasha and I have the door closed and locked. The neighbors have come and gone. It's late. I told everybody Aunt Jolita'd be home momentarily. The police don't ever show up. That man can get away with whatever he wants and he knows it.

Tasha and I go to bed by ourselves. It feels funny to do that without Mama home, like when you don't brush your teeth before bed and lying under the covers doesn't feel right. Tomorrow we have to go to school and tell everybody that Aunt Jolita is good to us, feeding us right and everything, so we don't go to foster care even for a week. I know kids in foster care. The project's bad. But foster care's worse.

When we get home from school, Aunt Jolita lets us in. She's been waxing the kitchen floor so it shines, and she's dressed in a torn pair of blue jeans and an old T-shirt instead of her party clothes.

"How's Mama?" I ask.

"Oh, pretty good," Jolita says, scrubbing hard at the tiles, black with tiny flecks of orange, yellow, and blue in them. She doesn't look at me, just at the floor.

"What's pretty good mean?"

"She has a concussion. That's when you hit your head. And she has to rest a few days. They'll be X-raying her foot this afternoon."

"When's she coming home?" I ask.

"She doesn't know yet."

"We usually have Kool-Aid after school," Tasha says.

"Is that so? Well, the floor's wet. You'll have to wait."

Tasha's scowling because she's trying not to cry. Everything feels so different with Mama gone.

"You quit that pouting, young lady," Jolita says, standing up and putting the bucket in the sink upside down to dry.

I want to smack her, I feel so mad. Instead, I turn around and go into my room. I'm breathing hard, thinking about last night and how they went out and left Mama hurt on the stairs like that. And Jolita never said she was sorry, either. Not to us, anyway.

Someone knocks at the door. When I look out from my bedroom, I see Trevor and Jolita talking together with the door open. Tasha's in the rocking chair, sucking on her fingers, not crying, though.

That's something. I wonder, what business has Trevor got with Jolita?

Suddenly he turns to me. "Can you come out?" he asks. "Me and Robert are getting a game up."

"No," I say. "I don't think so."

"What do you mean?" Jolita asks. "It's a nice day. Of course you can go out. I'll watch Tasha."

"You will?" I feel confused. Maybe I have this all wrong. Maybe Jolita *is* trying to be extra-nice, washing the floor and everything. "Okay, I guess."

"Come on, then," Trevor says. "We gotta hurry."

But when we get downstairs and out back, there's no one there. I don't see Robert or any other kids.

"Maybe they're waiting around front," Trevor says.

"There's no hoop around front," I say.

He pays me no attention and starts wandering around the front of the building, and I follow after. It's nice enough out, warm, with high thin milky clouds. A good sailor always looks at the sky. But those high thin clouds sometimes mean a rainstorm's coming in.

"You see those clouds?" I start to say. "Hey, Trevor . . ."

But Trevor's over at the curb and a Mercedes pulls up. The door opens. Radar man steps out.

"He was, too, with Darnell. My friend Robert told me," I hear Trevor saying to the man. "I swear."

"Come over here!" the man calls to me.

72

"Take this," he says to Trevor and stuffs some dollar bills in his hand. "Now get out of here."

Trevor shoves the money into his pocket and takes off, running, without looking at me. The man waits for me to come a little closer. I take one or two steps and stop. That's close enough.

"Your friend's a snitch," says the man. "You know what that is?"

"Someone who tells on people?"

"Right. But you're not a snitch, are you?"

"No," I mumble. I just want to get away. I don't want to get near the car.

"So you were with Darnell the other day, weren't you?"

I look at him, but I don't answer.

He folds his arms and smiles at me as if he likes what he sees. "I'm not going to hurt you. I just need to ask a few questions."

"Better ask Darnell, then," I say.

"Ahh. I can't. He's not around, you see. That's the problem."

I'm thinking fast now. How can I get out of this? I have to make him think that I'm trying to help him.

"Ask his mother. She'll know. He's real close with his mother." I know Darnell's mother doesn't know where he is. And Gabe won't let the radar man hurt his mother.

He thinks this over. "Is she home?"

"Yeah."

I act real patient, as if I've got all the time in the world. Neither one of us moves. Then he reaches into his pocket.

"Here's five dollars," he says. "You run up there and find out from her where Darnell is, and I'll give you ten more when you get back. All right?"

He stretches out his hand with the money. I don't move. I can be as stubborn as Tasha if I have to.

"No, thanks. I don't need your money," I say, polite as anything.

I turn around and start walking toward the building, as if I'm gonna go find Darnell's mother. She's home, too. Asleep or maybe just getting up for work. But I'm not going upstairs to their apartment. No way.

Instead, I walk through the dark lobby and out the back door. I slide under the fence and scramble down the embankment to the train tracks, and then I start running.

My feet are pounding along those railroad ties. Every step thuds in my chest. On and on I run, until I'm gasping for air and I have a cramp in my side. I run past the place where the old factories are. Past the place where I saw the ugly stray cat. To the bridge. I clamber up the embankment and slide my body in through the hole sideways, the way Darnell did.

"Darnell!" I call out. For a minute I think maybe

he's still in the hideout, but of course he's not. And then I start to cry.

Afterward, I lie still in the dark dirt on my chest, breathing hard. I think about all the things that happened, starting last night—Mama falling and the ambulance taking her away, and Jolita scrubbing the floor and then talking to Trevor. Darnell must have taken some of that man's money, for sure. But he must have had good reason for it. And now the man wants his money back. Well, I'm not helping him.

I realized then that Jolita knew the man was downstairs waiting for me. That was why she said I could go out. That was why she said she'd watch Tasha. Not because she was helping me out, but because she always does what her friends want her to do.

For the second time, I feel that hot shame about my family—about Jolita. The first time was when she wouldn't stand up to Georgina when we were trapped in the library. I gotta face the fact that we just don't matter to her. Not enough, anyway. If she won't help us out, if she won't protect us and keep us safe, we have to let her go.

Then, I guess because I'm a junebug, I ask myself a question: How come a boy like me is hiding in this dirty old hideout? It isn't right being in here, and I'm not going to do it. This is the one and only time I'm ever gonna use Darnell's hideout. I'm not gonna need it, that's why. And then, suddenly, I don't care if that new elderly care apartment is small and full of old people and the kids at King Elementary are snobs. Mama's got to take that new job, and I have to help her the best I can. I scramble out of the hole and brush the dirt off my clothes.

I can't wait to get home and call Mama at the hospital. And better yet, tomorrow I'll go down and see her. Hiding here in this hole? I'm just wasting my time.

When I get back to the apartment, I realize I don't have my key, so I pound on the door.

"Jolita?" I yell out. "Open up."

Bang, bang, bang on the door. But no one answers, and right away I get scared. What if the radar man came up here while I was gone? What if he and Jolita took Tasha away someplace? I feel just about sick to my stomach.

"Tasha!" I call out at the top of my lungs.

And then I can hear the bolts turning and the door opens a little. Tasha's standing there, tears covering her whole face. And she's all alone.

"It's okay now, Tasha," I say. "Don't worry."

I lead her over to the refrigerator and get out the Kool-Aid. Let's start this afternoon over again.

"You know what?" I say to her.

She looks at me but doesn't answer. She starts sipping on the Kool-Aid, though, orange this time.

"Tomorrow I'm going down to the hospital to visit

Mama and find out when she's coming home. You can stay with Harriet Ames. You won't have to stay with Aunt Jolita."

She nods her head. "Okay," she says.

For early dinner that afternoon, Harriet brings us a great big casserole of American chop suey, and then she sits with us while we eat and pours us milk and everything. It's almost as good as having Mama back.

Tasha eats a whole ton of food, but there's still a lot left. For dessert, we have a chocolate cake that Darnell's mother brings over. I watch her and Harriet Ames talking in the doorway in quiet voices. I know they're talking about Jolita.

Just then Jolita comes up the stairs and breezes into the apartment, throws her purse on the couch. "Hello, ladies," she says as she goes by them, cool as anything.

Then she walks right to the kitchen and cuts herself a piece of cake and sits down at the table with us, licking the frosting off her fingers. Harriet and Darnell's mother disappear down the hall.

Saturday, Aunt Jolita gets up early for a change. She's smoking cigarettes and drinking coffee. Tasha and I sit on the sofa and watch cartoons for almost two hours. Then Jolita says, "Move over, kids." She sits down and flips through the TV channels.

I get up and look around the apartment. All the

floors are cleaned and waxed now. Looks like she went on a cleaning fit. My sneakers squeak because the wax is so thick. The oven door and the toaster are gleaming. Looks to me as if nobody lives here. No kids, anyway. I like it better when everything looks kind of used.

I go stand in front of Jolita. She's staring hard at the home-shopping channel, using her coffee cup for an ashtray. I feel anger coming up from my feet into my mouth. I don't know what I'm going to say. But I have to make her see what she's done.

"Move out of the way, Junebug," she says. She wants to see how much some earrings cost.

"Did you wish for all this to happen?" I ask. "Did you wish for Mama to get hurt?"

She doesn't yell back at me like I expect. She just flicks off the TV, reaching the remote around my legs so I won't block the signal. I stand right where I am. She doesn't answer. Then I know she didn't wish it. She didn't wish for anything.

"I'm taking the bus down to the hospital. And Harriet Ames said she'd watch Tasha."

"Yeah, all right," she says, not looking at me, checking her nails.

"Then you can go out with your friends," I say. "Because that's all you want to do, anyway."

Her head is down. She nods without even arguing back. And suddenly I don't feel so mad at her. She looks so pitiful with those long red fingernails and all that clanky jewelry and no reason for any of it.

I flop down on the sofa beside her. "You got anything special you want to do?" I ask.

"No," she whispers back. "Nothing special."

I go down and wait at the bus stop on Waverly Avenue. The bus with the sign on it for Torey Hill Mall, Robert told me, that's the hospital one. I get on and drop my coins in. Smells like metal up front. Like a bunch of pennies got loose and ran all around the place, leaving a coppery smell behind.

I slip down onto a hard plastic seat. It's bright orange. The driver's wearing a blue uniform like a mailman's. The ladies have their shopping bags wedged between their feet. The bus lurches forward, rocking everybody. Their heads sway all at once, and off we go.

I watch rows of little stores slide past the window—Army/Navy, hardware, laundromat, corner grocery. I wonder if Darnell took a bus when he ran away. Or maybe a plane, he had so much money. I wonder if he misses us all and wishes he could come back. But maybe he went to California and he's doing fine. I catch myself staring sadly out the window. That's no good. I have to sit up straight and get ready to see Mama.

I look at the store windows. My birthday's next

Saturday, but I don't really want anything from a store. When I saw Mama lying on the stairs all crumpled up, I realized we can't stay the way we are. We can't end up like Aunt Jolita with nothing special in mind. Dressing up, smoking cigarettes, and that's all.

First thing I'm going to do is get ready for my birthday. We're gonna have a party. I lean back and read the ads that run along the ceiling of the bus. There's one for a ferryboat cruise to Smuggler's Cove. That ferryboat would be a great place to launch my flotilla. I memorize the phone number, because we're taking that boat, for sure. That ferry's going to be my party boat.

The hospital stop comes up after we pass Yale University. Robert's mother cleans there. Robert and I went with her once. Big, cold stone buildings looking like castles. College students skinny and hunched up, dragging their books around. They wear flappy clothes and look like some kind of weird birds. Storks, maybe. Or ostriches.

In front of the hospital, the bus door hisses open and I leap for the curb. The sign over the door says NEW HAVEN HOSPITAL.

Mama's in room 713. That means the seventh floor, but it's not so bad getting up there because the elevator works just fine. All kinds of nurses and visitors get in with me, even two men nurses. We stand there, quiet, working our way up higher and higher. I watch the numbers light up yellow, one at a time,

80

above the door. No one makes a sound. How come? Sure isn't like the project elevator. Are these folks mad, or what?

It's so quiet I think someone's going to throw me out for sure. But nobody looks at me one way or the other. I get out on the seventh floor just as I'd planned.

I find Mama's room pretty quick and peek in at the door. The lady by the window, she has piles of flowers heaped up all over the place and a silvery balloon tied to the drawer handle. She's all dolled up in a pink nightie. In the other bed, Mama's lying still like a sad white lump of covers. No flowers. No balloon. Just one big get-well card and me sneaking in.

"Hey, Mama!"

"Junior!"

She struggles to sit up, excited. "Wait. I have to make the bed sit me up."

She pushes a button and the bed slowly rises in the back.

"Where's everybody else? Did Harriet bring you?"

"I took the bus," I say. "Harriet's got Tasha."

Mama starts to say something, but then stops. She frowns and shakes her head, but then she holds her head real still for a minute. It looks like maybe she's dizzy. I hold still, too, figuring it might help.

"Who sent you that great big card?" I ask.

"People at work. Look, they all signed it."

Mama hands it to me so I can see.

"That's nice." I hand it back.

"Junior?" Mama says. Then she stops. She sets the card real carefully on the roll-around table next to the plastic water jug.

"What?"

I start to get nervous. Something big's coming. Maybe she can't come home. Maybe they have to amputate her toes or something. I get a little shiver.

Mama starts folding the edge of the white blanket in creases like a fan until she has a pile of them stacked up. Then she lets go and starts folding all over again.

"Yeah?" I say.

"This morning, I called my supervisor at the nursing home."

"Yeah?"

"I told her I'd take that job with the group apartments. I told her I'd be the resident supervisor."

Mama looks at me.

"Oh," I say. And I let out a big sigh. That's good, then. Already, in my mind, I can see myself saying goodbye to Robert and I can see him going off with Trevor to do I don't know what. I remember Mama being driven away in the ambulance and that man trying to give me money.

"That's good," I say.

She smiles at me.

"There isn't room for Aunt Jolita over there?" I ask.

"No," she says, real quiet.

Her lips are pressed in. We look at the lumpy white blanket, thinking.

"Think she'll get her own apartment?" I ask.

"Not without a job," Mama says. "I guess she can stay with her friends until she figures a few things out."

I nod, not sure what to say. There isn't an answer to Aunt Jolita right now, I guess. Time to change the subject. Didn't I come here to plan my birthday party?

"So," I say, grinning at Mama. "When are you getting out?"

"A few more days," she says, still looking fretful.

"Well, you better hurry up. Next Saturday is my birthday, in case you forgot with all this excitement. Only seven more shopping days."

"What? I thought you—"

"We're taking a boat ride."

"We are?"

"Yep. We're taking the ferry ride over to Smuggler's Cove for a picnic."

"What a nice idea!" she says.

I know she likes picnics. I do, too.

"There's just one thing. Don't forget to buy me those corks."

She laughs. The lady in the next bed looks over and smiles at her. I guess she's glad to see Mama laugh.

"You're not leaving much to chance, are you?" she says.

"Nope."

Nine

Sunday I spend finishing my notes. Then I put all fifty of them in the bottles, even the little tiny perfume bottles. I line them up neatly under my bed, ready and waiting.

Wednesday afternoon, Harriet drives me and Tasha down to the hospital in her old green Hornet. We go up to room 713, and there's Mama sitting on the edge of her bed, packed and ready to go. She's wearing a cast on her foot. It's a big, clunky thing with gray Velcro straps holding all the padding and supports in place. She gets around pretty well with it.

Until we get home to the stairs.

Harriet laughs. "Looks like your mother's going to have to use the elevator for once."

Mama frowns. "I can walk up, Harriet."

"Oh, no, you don't," Harriet says. She pushes the button. "You're staying with me."

So Mama and Harriet take the elevator. Tasha and I run for the staircase. We're going to race them up to the ninth floor.

We're ahead of them at the sixth floor, but after that we don't have a chance. They're just opening the door to our apartment when Tasha and I burst out of the stairwell, huffing and puffing.

Inside, I flop onto the sofa upside down and let the blood rush back to my brain.

Meanwhile, Harriet helps Mama get unpacked. "You let your mother rest here on the sofa, June-bug," Harriet says, shooing me out of the way. Then she arranges the pillows so Mama can stretch out on the sofa and prop her foot up.

I'm so glad to have Mama home, I don't care where I sit.

That night, Mama and I discuss my birthday plans. Jolita's home, but she and Mama have hardly said a word to each other.

"Remember," I tell Mama, "I don't need a cake. Cupcakes are better for a picnic. We'll need ten of 'em."

"Yes, sir!" Mama salutes me from the sofa.

She should have said, "Aye-aye," but I let her get away with it this time.

Jolita comes out of the bathroom.

"What picnic? I don't think I can go."

I go right over to the bathroom. I'm gonna nip this

mutiny in the bud. "It's my birthday, so you have to come."

She doesn't answer. Instead, she's looking in the mirror, reaching for her curling iron to put the finishing touches on her hair. I switch off the light from outside the door, so she's got no power.

"Junebug!" she hollers. "Turn on that light!"

"You didn't answer me," I say.

"Answer you about what?"

She hasn't even been listening. All the time I've been talking, she's been thinking about herself. I guess it doesn't matter much if she moves out.

"Nothing," I say.

I turn the light back on and wander over to the sofa. Mama rubs my shoulder and I sit back, relaxed. I'm glad she's home.

My birthday at last! I get up early and see my bag of corks sitting on the table with a ribbon around it. Yeah!

After breakfast, we get the picnic packed. Cupcakes, candles, juice, grapes, sandwiches, chips. Nothing left out. Harriet gives us a ride down to the ferry terminal in time for the ten o'clock boat. Tasha and I are in the back seat with two trash bags full of bottles.

We struggle out of the car and say goodbye. Mama finds a long, red bench to sit down on and gives me money to go buy tickets.

The ferry sits tied up to the dock with some nice thick ropes. Everything's painted fresh with heavy, shiny paint. The smokestack is bright red, with a wide yellow stripe. The ferry's clean and cheerful, like a party hat.

The crew is getting ready to get the boat going. They swing on and off, doing their work, all casual. One man goes right up to the wheelhouse in front of the smokestack to talk to the captain. Now they're hauling out the ramp for the passengers to get on. That's us.

We have tickets for the two-hour harbor cruise, all around the harbor and then a short stop at Smuggler's Cove and back. By the time we get done, my flotilla of bottles is going to be floating off in every direction, its journey begun.

"Come on," I say. "They're taking tickets. Let's go."

Mama heaves her leg down and takes the picnic basket with Tasha holding the handle. I've got the trash bags, clanking along beside them.

All of a sudden, Tasha hangs back, pulling on Mama's arm as if she doesn't want to go. I turn around and give her a look that says, "You better get yourself on this boat and fast!" But that just makes her hang back even more. Everyone has gotten on board except us.

"Come on, Tasha," says Mama. "Don't ruin Junior's birthday."

I never thought that she might be scared of the ferryboat. She shakes her head, about to cry. Quickly, I reach into my trash bag and hunt around for one of my best bottles. A light green, rectangle-shaped one with a tall neck. It says 1894 on the bottom. Darnell's grandfather gave it to me. I hand it to her.

"Tasha, come on. You can put my most magic bottle out to sea. You launch it for me, okay?"

Tasha nods and takes the bottle. I know she'll help me out, just the way I'll help her out any time she needs it. She holds the bottle real tight and shuts her eyes while she crosses the gangplank with Mama. There. Now we're set.

We go and sit on the big red toolbox in the stern. The engine's running, vibrating the deck so that my feet tingle. White foam is churning up behind the boat.

I survey the view and check the weather. Warm sun is sitting on top of my head, and a cool breeze is on my face. The sky is big and blue, with a couple of white clouds floating along up there. Big gray seagulls are perched on the railing, just the way they're supposed to be. This is the best!

Then the horn gives a loud blast! It goes right through me. Whoa! None of us is ready for that. Tasha's lips start to quiver and her eyes look worried. The boat shudders and shakes and begins to back up. A man on the dock unties the big ropes and tosses them to the crew, and they wind them up in big coils.

"We're moving!" I shout.

Mama stands Tasha on top of the tool chest so she can see and holds her tight. And we chug out into the harbor.

The harbor's full of boats—motorboats, fishing boats, marine patrol, sailboats. We even get right up close to an oil tanker, rising up high like a big metal mountain. It's huge! I get so busy running from railing to railing that I almost forget why I came.

"You better get started," Mama reminds me.

I open the first trash bag and take out the old glass Coke bottle, carved like a statue. My note's leaning against the side. I push the cork in extra-tight, squeeze the bottle, close my eyes, and wish real hard.

Then I take the bottle and throw it in a big high arc. Splash! For one second, it sinks down out of sight. Oh no! My stomach tightens up. The bottles have to float. They have to. I clench my fists. Come on, come on. I wish that bottle up to the surface.

There it is! I see it bobbing up, riding halfway under, going up and down over the little waves in the harbor.

Then Tasha throws her bottle. She climbs up on the tool chest to watch.

"Hey, look," a man yells from the other side of the ferry. "A message in a bottle."

"Yeah," I say to Tasha. "And it's time for another one."

This time I get out a tall green bottle, deep green. I toss it out. Then a big clear jug, the kind that holds apple cider. It's got a big old cork in the top and my little wish folded up inside. The jug floats on its side, riding the waves.

Going out to the island, I toss out half the bottles.

After we tie up at the dock, we get a half hour to get off the boat and walk around. No way we're getting off, between Mama's foot and my wanting to stay on board. So we sit on the tool chest and have our picnic and eat all the cupcakes except for two. Then Mama and Tasha start singing "Happy Birthday" pretty loud.

I hear someone clapping. It's the captain. He comes on over and shakes my hand. "How old are you?" he asks.

"I'm ten."

"Want to come up and look at the wheelhouse? You and your little sister?"

Tasha doesn't, but I sure do. I go up the little steps into the wheelhouse. The captain's seat is way up high. He's got a big steering wheel and a radar screen. I climb into the seat and survey the view. Finally he says I have to get down, because the other passengers are coming back to the boat.

"Thanks a lot," I say.

He waves good bye, and then he gets busy. He has a lot to do.

On the way back to the ferry terminal, I toss out the rest of the bottles, one by one. By now there's a crowd of passengers to cheer me on. Everybody's hanging onto the railing, hollering and laughing. It's fun to watch the bottles mark the trail behind us.

At one point, a little sailboat crosses the waves behind the ferry's stern. I'm up so high that I can look right down into the boat. An old guy and a little kid are sailing along, and the little kid's got ahold of the rope and the tiller. The old man's just leaning back, relaxing. The kid sees me watching him and he waves at me. I wave back. Then I go back to tossing bottles.

Soon there's only one left. It should be one of those tiny little perfume bottles that I was saving for last. But I can't find it. I look through the plastic bags and the picnic basket. I look around the deck. Some of the passengers look, too. But we can't find it anywhere.

I know it doesn't matter. I have forty-nine bottles already on their way. I know one more won't make a difference.

As the ferry nears the dock, I start feeling pretty sad. I'm leaning up against the railing, my head resting on the cold white metal.

Mama gets up and comes over. "Big day?" she asks.

"Yeah."

I'm thinking maybe I shouldn't have come out here like this. Getting my head full of waves and birds and sea air. Seeing that little kid sailing along behind us. Now my wish is turning into something painful and achy. Now I've got my own kind of seasickness.

I have to get back out here someday. But who's going to read the message in the bottles? Who? Not in this day and age. Who's going to call up and say, "Yeah, Junebug. You can come on my boat."

Nobody. That's who.

Tears sting my eyes. I turn away from Mama. I know she works real hard for us, and it was hard for her coming on the boat with her foot hurt.

She bends over. "Once you let yourself get your hopes up, it starts to hurt worse inside," she says. "Is that it?"

I nod. And two tears fall out. Big ones, like they've been holding on a long, long time.

"That's okay," she says, and hugs me. "Your bottles are going to work just fine."

The ferry chugs into the harbor real slow, making no waves out the back. We come alongside the dock, and the deckhands toss the ropes ashore nice and easy. They lasso the metal pilings, and we land.

Mama's putting all our stuff, jackets and chip bags, into the basket. I feel like Tasha, hanging back, droopy and sad.

We line up with everybody else at the gangplank, waiting to get off. But just as we start up the ramp,

Mama can't find Tasha. She turns her head back and forth, looking for her.

"Maybe she got ahead of us," I say.

Mama hurries up the gangplank as fast as she can and looks around the ferry terminal. I glance quickly around the boat and follow after her. It sure isn't like Tasha to disappear. What if she fell into the water?

Then I see her. She's walking by herself up the gangplank, grinning from ear to ear at me and Mama, the last one off the boat.

"Get yourself over here!" Mama says, relieved and angry all at once. "Where were you?"

Tasha shakes her head, smiling as if she's got a big secret.

"Happy birthday, Junebug," she says, and skips to Mama's side.

Ten

Back at the apartment, our bedroom looks lots bigger without the bottles lined up on the windowsill and the dresser. It also looks empty. I don't usually give stuff away on my birthday. Maybe I should have kept my wish here to keep me company when I get sad and lonely. Hug it close, polish it, and let it sit where no one can see it.

But good old Junebug can't leave things alone. I just had to go and float my bottles out to sea. I bet people take the cork off and laugh when they read my message. Then they take the bottle home for an extra nickel. Maybe they even keep the cork, but that's all.

Sunday, Monday, and Tuesday go by. Rainy, cold, and dull. The tar out back is full of puddles. Walls of the gun factory are stained black with water. The chain-link fence has rust weeping out of it, as if even the metal got sad.

The apartment is a mess. Mama's been collecting boxes and newspapers so we can move. She's got piles of stuff stacked up all over the place. Boxes are everywhere. I feel like kicking them.

Then, Wednesday night at supper, the phone rings.

"That's for me," Jolita says. She jumps up and hurries to the phone, pushing her shoulder in close, all cuddly with the receiver.

Then she turns around, cold. "Junebug, it's for you," she says, sitting down to eat.

My eyes shoot open wide. I stare at Mama, frozen to my seat.

"Better find out who it is," she says.

"It could be Darnell."

"Could be."

I pick up the receiver. "Hello?"

"Hello, Reeve?"

"Yes?" I squeak, my mouth dry as anything.

"This is the ferry captain. You must be the young man who sent the messages in the bottles. Your little sister gave me a tiny bottle before we docked the other day, but all over the harbor, people are finding your messages. Looks like you really want to be a sailor."

"I do!"

I turn around and stare at Mama. They're sitting at the table, looking at me.

"Well, I talked to a friend of mine at Fair Harbor Boatyard. A couple folks over there picked up your messages, too. My buddy, Ron, over there said he'd give you some sailing lessons in return for some chores done around the boatyard. Think you'd be interested?''

"I can do chores,'' I say really quick. I want him to know I know how important it is to keep things shipshape.

"Great!'' The captain laughs. "Ron's going to call you, but, here, let me give you his number.''

"Okay.'' I start fumbling around for a pencil, and finally Mama has to come over and help out.

I race to the table and grab Tasha's arm. "I got a job at the boatyard with some sailing lessons!''

Tasha grins back at me with a wide, milky-mustache grin.

"Hey! Did you give the captain that little teeny bottle?''

"Yeah,'' she says. "Just in case.''

Eleven

We've been packing for real because we have to move on Friday night. Mama waited so long to decide about the job that we have no more time to waste. No big deal, though. I only have some clothes and toys.

Darnell's big brother, Gabe, is going to get some friends to help us. We're going to do it in one trip with a car and a pickup truck. We aren't going far. It's only a couple of miles across town.

Jolita is stalking around the apartment as if she doesn't even know us. Maybe she doesn't. She's going to be staying at Georgina's for a while. Is that a dumb idea, or what? Right now she's supposed to be helping us pack. She wraps our cereal bowls in newspaper and jams them down in the box. She shoves the toaster and radio in on top. Careless and nasty. Her same old self.

All the while, Tasha's sitting in Mama's rocking

chair, sucking on her fingers. She's rocking and holding her doll babies, watching the couch go out the door. Good thing the elevator's working today.

Jolita's got two suitcases ready to go and a big box with all her makeup and bathroom stuff. Georgina shows up in the doorway and stands there, looking. I have nothing to say to her. Instead, I go into the bedroom, where Gabe's taking apart our beds with a screwdriver.

"Georgina's up here, standing around with nothing to do," I say.

Gabe smiles at me and shakes his head. For a second he looks like Darnell, and my throat hurts.

"You hear from Darnell yet?"

"Nope," says Gabe. "Not yet."

He lifts the side of the bed rail and stands it against the wall. Then he starts working on the other side.

"Think he's doing okay?" I ask in a tiny voice.

"Who, Darnell?" Gabe says. "Of course he is. You don't need to worry about Darnell, Junebug. You go on and worry about yourself."

"Okay."

I like watching him take the beds apart. It looks pretty easy. Bet I could do it next time.

"Here," says Gabe. "Think you could take the side rails out in the hall? I could use some more room in here."

Those metal sides are heavier than they look, but I drag them into the hall, and pretty soon we're in the elevator with the last boxes. Jolita follows, taking the stairs.

Outside, we walk over to the truck and load it up. Gabe is driving us in the car. His two friends are in the truck.

"Well," says Mama, turning to Jolita. "You come on over and visit us real soon."

Jolita seems kind of mad at us for leaving her. She smiles at her girlfriend, Georgina, and folds her arm across her stomach. "All right," she says. "Maybe."

"When she gets around to it," Georgina says, and collapses, giggling.

Mama starts to say something, but Gabe reaches over and takes her arm. "Let's go," he says, leading Mama to the car. She's still got her cast on, but she's walking better every day.

"Bye," I call out to Jolita.

"Bye, Junebug. Be good," she says.

I look back. Georgina's laughing and touching Jolita's arm as if she owns her now that Mama's out of the way.

Jolita sees me looking. "Bye," she yells again.

"Bye," I yell back.

But Tasha doesn't say a word.

Our new apartment is across town. It's light out in the evening now, and patches of grass here and there are a soft, new green. It's baseball time. Baby leaves on the trees are the color of lime Kool-Aid. We drive past the Town Hall and head west, past the hospital.

On a little dead-end street, there's a brand-new set of buildings, little groups of apartments for the elderly. Some have cement ramps up to the doors. The ramps would be good for skateboarding, but I doubt there will be a lot of kids coming around here. I don't see a hoop anywhere.

We have our own driveway for the pickup truck to pull into. Makes it a lot easier to unload, getting up close like that.

We get all the boxes inside, and the TV and the beds. Gabe gets the beds put together again, and lays the mattresses on them. Then he and his friends are ready to leave. Mama gives them money for a great big pizza. They wave and drive off.

Mama and Tasha and I stand all alone in our new living room, looking at each other as if we don't know what to do. It sure is awful quiet on this side of town. I can't hear any sirens or the soft roar of the eighteen-wheel trailer trucks on I-95. No doors slamming, no radios on. Nothing.

All of a sudden, I look down. "Hey!" I say.

I just noticed that I'm standing on brand-new orange carpet. That strikes me funny, and I have to laugh. I'm not used to carpeting.

"I don't know about you," Mama says, but she's laughing, too.

"Tomorrow is it! My big day down at the boat-yard," I announce.

"Yeah, it is," says Mama. "And I have a lot to do between now and then. Here, take a pile of these sheets. Let's get unpacked."

She doesn't know it, but she's talking to Captain McClain.